OUTDOOR EXPLORER

I SEE FLOWERS

by Tim Mayerling

TABLE OF CONTENTS

tadpole
books

I SEE FLOWERS

I see yellow sunflowers.

daisy

I see white daisies.

I see pink roses.

I see orange lilies.

I see purple lilacs.

poppy

I see red poppies.

What colors do you see?

WORDS TO KNOW

daisies

lilacs

lilies

poppies

roses

sunflowers

INDEX

OUTDOOR EXPLORER

Look up! You can see trees and birds.
Look down! You can see plants and rocks.
Explore the world around you with these
fun books. Have you read them all?

B

F&P Text Level Gradient™

Officially Leveled by **Fountas & Pinnell**

LOOK FOR OTHER TITLES IN THE SERIES:

IL: PreK–1   ATOS: 0.9   GRL: B

ISBN 978-1-62031-948-2

90000

9 781620 319482

jump!

www.jumplibrary.com
www.jumplibrary.com/teachers